To all those like Roberta who care about the millions of kinds of other creatures that share this wonderful planet with us —**C.M.**

For Maggie, whose heart is always set to "rescue" —**L.R.C.**

Published by Roaring Brook Press
Roaring Brook Press is a division of Holtzbrinck Publishing Holdings Limited Partnership
120 Broadway, New York, NY 10271 · mackids.com

Library of Congress Control Number: 2020914902
ISBN 978-1-250-24671-4

Our books may be purchased in bulk for promotional, educational, or business use.
Please contact your local bookseller or the Macmillan Corporate and Premium Sales Department
at (800) 221-7945 ext. 5442 or by email at MacmillanSpecialMarkets@macmillan.com.

First edition, 2021 · Book design by Mercedes Padró
The illustrations in this book were created with gouache, colored pencils, charcoal,
and markers and finished digitally.
Printed in China by RR Donnelley Asia Printing Solutions Ltd., Dongguan City, Guangdong Province

1 3 5 7 9 10 8 6 4 2

The Rescuer of Tiny Creatures

words by
CURTIS MANLEY

pictures by
LUCY RUTH CUMMINS

Roaring Brook Press
New York

I rescue tiny creatures.
It's a special job.

A job no one
else seems
to care
about.

So many tiny creatures get into trouble every day.

They get flipped on their backs and can't turn over.

They end up in places with nothing to eat.

They crawl only halfway across the
sidewalk before the day gets warm.

Tiny creatures need friends who can
rescue and understand them.

"Ms. Williams! Roberta has been picking up worms again!" says Luis.

"Oh, Roberta ... don't touch anything!
I'll turn on the water for you."

"No one has ever been harmed
by earthworm slime," I say,
but no one hears me.

But my cat understands,
and she's a good helper.
She follows small, moving things.
She points out moths.
She corners spiders.

My little brother helps, too.

"Yuck!"

I carry the ladybug outside.
"Fly away home," I whisper.

And it does.

The best rescues were when I got to
know a tiny creature before letting it go.

The millipede was smooth and dry,

and it curled into a spiral when I picked it up.

On my hand, it went exploring
with its bobbing feelers,
but I couldn't feel it at all—even with all
those stomping feet.

Did it even know my hand was alive?

But some rescues came with rules I had to follow.
Like when I found a baby snail in a bunch of radishes.

Mom said, "That thing can eat whatever it wants in the
front yard, but it is NOT welcome in the garden, young lady."

And one time, my effort
was not appreciated.

I picked up a dragonfly that was
flopping around on the ground.
It bit me, and I dropped it.

"No fair!" I said.
"I was trying to help!"

With some rescues I was just too late.

A beetle
slowed down . . .

and stopped.

A bumblebee
struggled

in the grass.

All I could do was put them where no
one would step on them.

They were still there the next day, not
moving, so I kept them.

They're so beautiful!

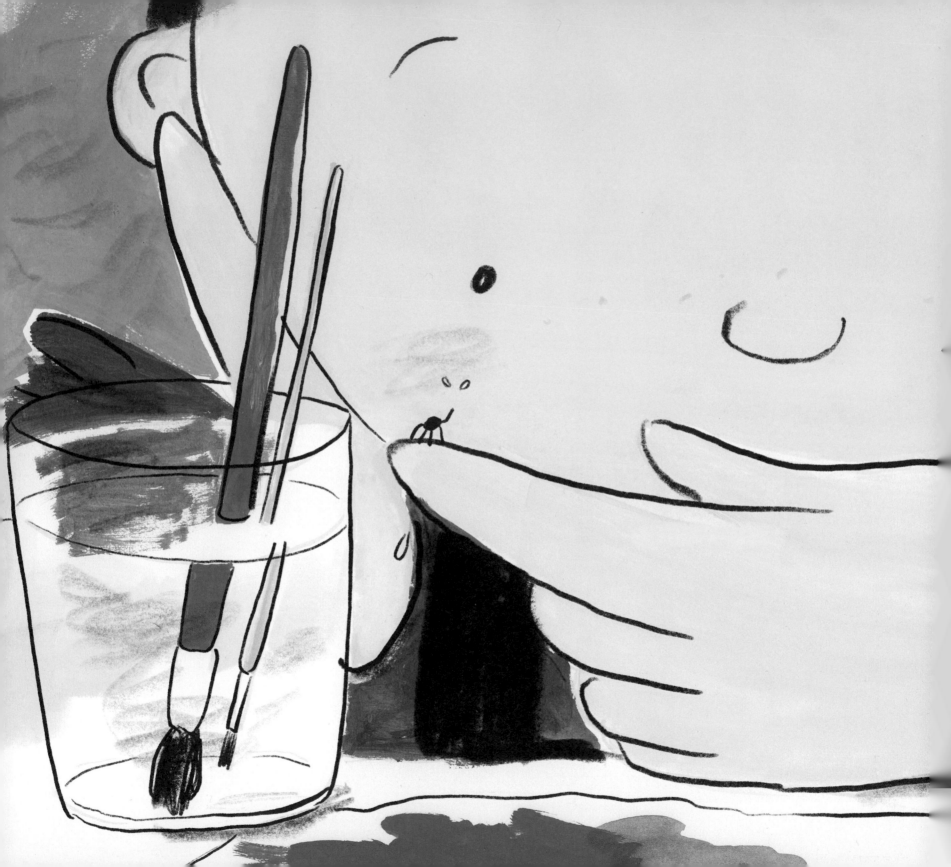

Most rescues are easy, like with
a baby spider. It's so tiny—just a stripy
speck with legs.

But some rescues seem impossible.
Like when someone yells,

and everyone crowds
into the far corner
because one wall of the room
is covered with hundreds
of stripy specks . . .

There are so many of them,
I wish I had twenty hands.

And then I realize . . .

. . . I do!

"Who wants the spiders out of here right away?" I ask.
Everyone raises a hand.

"Okay," I say. "Everyone has to help. Get a sheet of
paper and Maria will show you how to fold it."

Soon we have eleven little origami boxes—and I show
everyone how to get the spider babies to drop inside.

We line up and carry the spiders outside.

"Set your boxes along the wall and open them," I say.
"The little spiders want to climb up."

"Why do they want to climb?" asks Luis.

"You won't believe me if I tell you," I mumble.
But someone hears me.

"Roberta?" Ms. Williams prompts.

I take a deep breath.

"They'll climb all the way up to the
roof. They'll stand on tippy-toes
and unfurl their spider silk.
And then the breeze
will float them like balloons
to new homes far away."

Everyone is quiet.

They stare at me as if
I am a spider.

And then everyone is talking.

Ms. Williams claps her hands.

"Let's all thank Roberta and Maria for showing us what to do."

And everyone says,

"THANK YOU!"

Everyone.

"I want to take these two home with me. To show my brother. And then they can climb our house!"

The next day at recess,
Maria comes over to me and sits close.

"Last week I found a honeybee in the grocery store,"
she whispers. "It was so cold it could hardly move!"

"What did you do?" I ask.

"I put it in an egg carton and carried it outside.
Then I told it, *Stay out of the store, Fluffy—it's not warm
enough for you!*"

"You named it Fluffy?"

"I did."

"You know," I say,
"if you and I teamed up,
we could rescue . . ."

Maria's eyes grow wide.
". . . *bigger* creatures!"

"Birds and lizards," I say.

"Pandas and pangolins," says Maria.

"Polar bears?"

"Rhinos and elephants!"

"No, that's too big for just two of us."

"I think I know who might help," I say,
and we both look over at Luis.

ROBERTA'S FAVORITE TINY CREATURES WORTH RESCUING

EARTHWORM

I've lost count of all the earthworms I've seen on drying sidewalks and moved into the grass. But no earthworm has ever seen me—because they don't actually have eyes! They can sense light, though, so if you go out on a wet night, you can watch earthworms yank themselves back into their burrows to hide from your flashlight. As earthworms dig through the soil, they create tunnels that bring air and water underground, and their poop is rich in nutrients plants need.

LADYBIRD BEETLE ("LADYBUG")

Ladybugs are so pretty, with their bright red or orange bodies speckled with black dots! Most ladybugs are good beetles to have in your yard or garden. They and their larvae, which look like tiny orange-and-black alligators, eat aphids and other plant pests. Adult ladybugs survive winter by hiding in cracks and going dormant; when they wake up, they're some of the first insects to appear in the spring.

MILLIPEDE

It's fun to touch a millipede and watch it curl into a little spiral and hug itself with all its tiny legs—but I don't do it very often, because it isn't polite. The name *millipede* means "thousand feet," but no species of millipede has more than 750 feet. Millipedes are scavengers and eat tiny bits of plant debris they find on the ground.

Centipedes may look similar to millipedes, but they have longer legs and can move very fast. Centipedes hunt tiny pests; they can also bite people. Some are poisonous, so don't pick them up.

SNAIL

I like when a snail unfurls its tentacles and eyestalks and then begins to glide around on its one large, wet foot. A snail's tongue works like a tiny cheese grater to grind up plant leaves and stems. If you listen very closely as it eats, you might hear a sound like the crunching of tiny stalks of celery.

DRAGONFLY

Dragonflies can't actually hurt you much if they bite—it's more like a little pinch. But it really surprised me! Dragonflies eat smaller insects such as flies and mosquitoes. They are skillful hunters, partly due to their big compound eyes with many thousands of individual lenses.

GROUND BEETLE

I'm sure that ground beetles have no idea how beautiful they are! Their shiny black or brown exterior often has a metallic sheen of purple, orange, or green. They hunt at night and feed on many types of pests.

BUMBLEBEE

Bumblebees do seem to *bumble* from flower to flower, but they fly well and are clumsy only sometimes. Bumblebees are important pollinators and can be more active in cooler weather than honeybees. Bumblebees build nests in holes in the ground, under moss, or in the grass. Each nest has only about 50 to 500 bees—much smaller than a honeybee hive.

GARDEN SPIDER

I'm a bit afraid of spiders—especially big ones—but I know that most spiders can't bite or harm humans. (The ones in North America that are dangerous are the black widow and the brown recluse.) Spiders catch and eat many of the small flying insects that humans consider pests.

When spiders take to the air to find new homes, it is called ballooning (even though the "balloon" is a strand of silk and is not actually inflated). Large numbers of ballooning spiders have been observed landing on ships at sea and high up on skyscrapers.

Although all spiders can spin spider silk, many species don't build webs; they hunt by jumping onto—and grabbing—their tiny prey.

HONEYBEE

Honeybees always seem so busy! But I think that's because they rest only in their hives, where we can't see them. The honeybee was domesticated thousands of years ago and is now making honey on all the continents except Antarctica. Honeybees are also important pollinators for crops like almonds and apples, and for many types of flowers.

KRAKEN

If they actually exist, kraken are not tiny but really big! Is a kraken a bigger octopus than has ever been seen? Or a gigantic squid? Or something else entirely? No one knows . . . If there are lots of kraken in the ocean, people would be seeing them all the time—so if they do exist they must be rare, and if we find one in trouble we should rescue it. Somehow!

MARIA'S ORIGAMI BOX WITH LOCKABLE LID

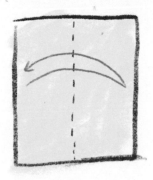

1. Fold an 8.5" × 11" sheet of paper in half lengthwise. Unfold.

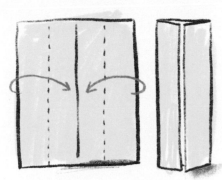

2. Bring longer edges to meet the center crease. Leave folded.

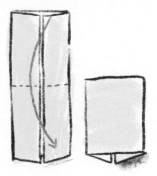

3. Fold in half from the top down. Leave folded.

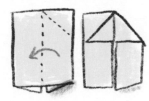

4. Squash-in the top right corner while folding right side over left side.

5. Unfold.

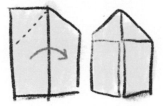

6. Squash-in the top left corner while folding left side over right side.

7. Unfold.

8. Bring vertical sides of upper layer to meet the center crease.

9. Turn over and repeat step 8 on other layer.

10. Fold upper layer toward top by thirds.

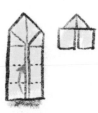

11. Turn over and repeat step 10 on other layer.

12. Unflatten the box: Carefully pull the handle flaps away from each other, then push up the pointed bottom to make the base flat.

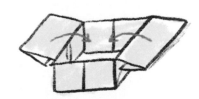

13. Bend the flaps so they cover the opening.

14. Hold the handle flaps together and press them down into the box to lock it closed.